IAN OLIO

# DID DRAGONS EVER EXIST?

## For Kids Ages 4-9

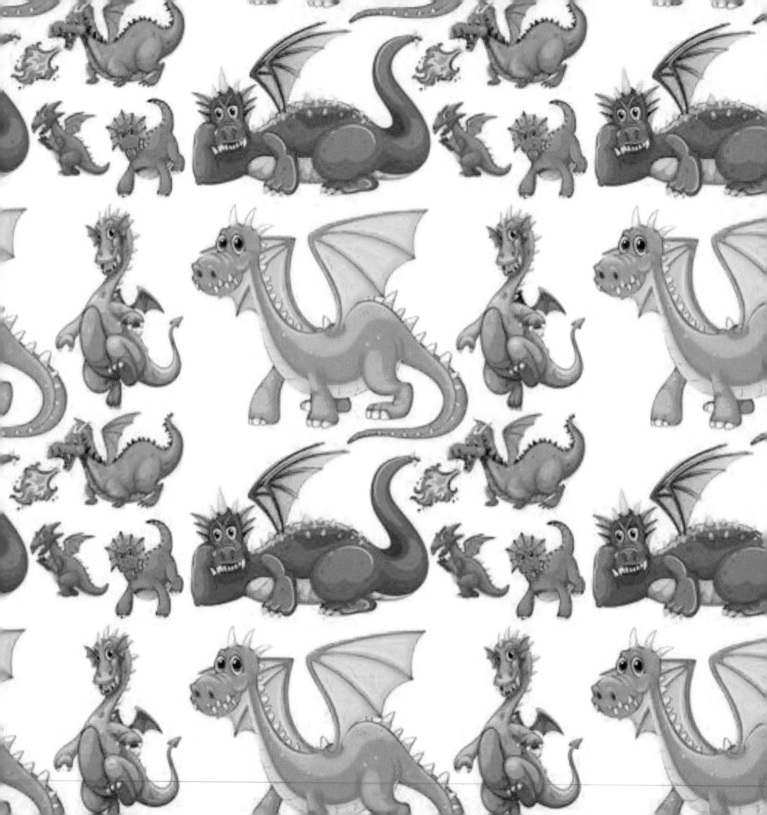

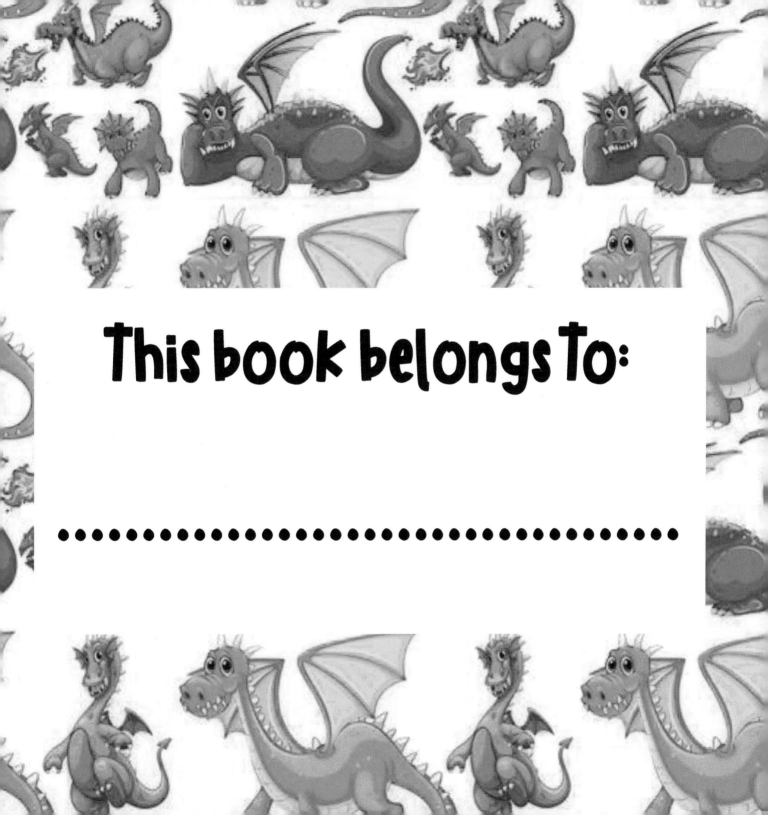

# This book belongs to:

...............................................

Hello friend!
When you hear the word "dragon",
what do you think of?

...a lizard-like creature with clawed feet that flies and has a long neck with three heads!

Where do all these myths
of dragons come from?

# Did the real the dragons really exist on Earth?

Fire-breathing dragons never actually existed. Dragons aren't real but there are stories about them everywhere all around the world.

The main reason is all those big mysterious bones that people were occasionally digging up for thousands of years.

Experts can only suppose which ancient animal bones inspired the first dragon legends.

But they are almost sure that ancient people were digging up dinosaur bones.

It kind of makes sense since dinosaurs basically look like giant lizards.

Dragons can be mean and destructive,
but there are stories where they can be
very helpful and protective too.

In different cultures and myths dragons have the head of an elephant, lion, snake or a bird.

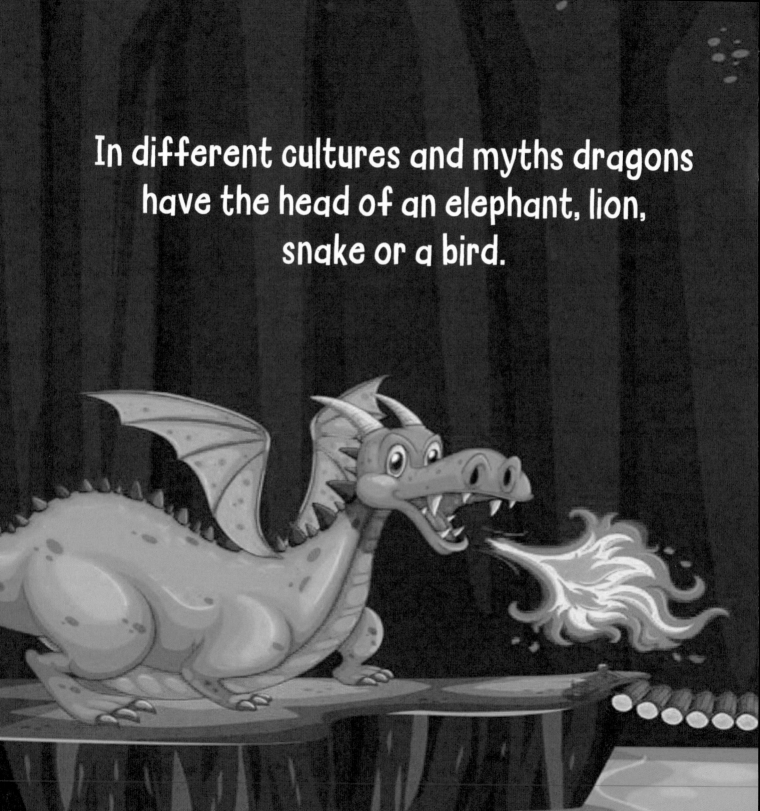

They can be all sorts of colors: black,
green, red, even blue, yellow
or white.

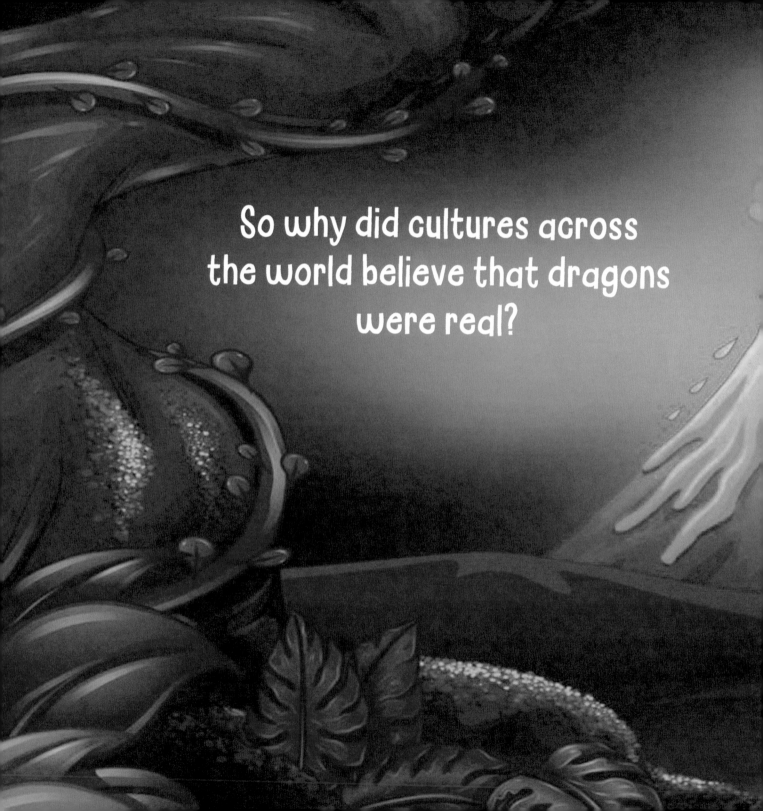

So why did cultures across the world believe that dragons were real?

They were finding giant bones
of the creatures that looked a lot like
fierce flying snakes or lizards...

And you know what?
maybe they weren't that
far off.

Hope you learned something new today.
See you next time!